Library of Congress Control Number: 2015039392

ISBN: 978-1-4197-2117-5

Text and illustrations copyright © 2014 Editions MeMo
English translation copyright © 2016 Harry N. Abrams, Inc.
Book design by Alyssa Nassner

Originally published in French in 2014 under the title *1,2,3 banquise* by éditions MeMo.

Printed and bound in China
10 9 8 7 6 5 4 3 2 1

For bulk discount inquiries, contact specialsales@abramsbooks.com.

ABRAMS
THE ART OF BOOKS SINCE 1949

115 West 18th Street
New York, NY 10011
www.abramsbooks.com

ONE
VERY BIG
BEAR

Written by **ALICE BRIÈRE-HAQUET**

Illustrated by **OLIVIER PHILIPPONNEAU** and **RAPHAËLE ENJARY**

Abrams Appleseed
New York

ONE white bear
stood on some ice.
"I'm very big!" he said.
"I'm almost a giant!"

TWO walrus swam up.
"Oh, Bear," they said.
"You're not *that* big."

"Look at this:

ONE

+ ONE

We **TWO** are just

as big as you!"

THREE foxes scampered by.

"Oh, Bear," they said.

"You silly thing!"

"Look at this:

ONE

+ ONE

+ ONE

We **THREE** are just

as big as you!"

FOUR sea lions joined the fun.

"Oh, Bear," they said.

"Stop showing off!"

"Look at this:

ONE

+ ONE

+ ONE

+ ONE

We **FOUR** are just
as big as you!"

FIVE penguins waddled past.

"Oh, Bear," they said.

"You make us laugh!"

"Look at this:

ONE

+ ONE

+ ONE

+ ONE

+ ONE

We **FIVE** are just
as big as you!"

SIX sardines joined in as well.

"Oh, Bear," they said.

"Don't be so foolish!"

"Look at this:

ONE

+ ONE

+ ONE

+ ONE

+ ONE

+ ONE

We **SIX** are just

as big as you!"

Foolish? thought the bear.
Then he had a very smart idea.
SIX sardines were the
perfect size for breakfast!